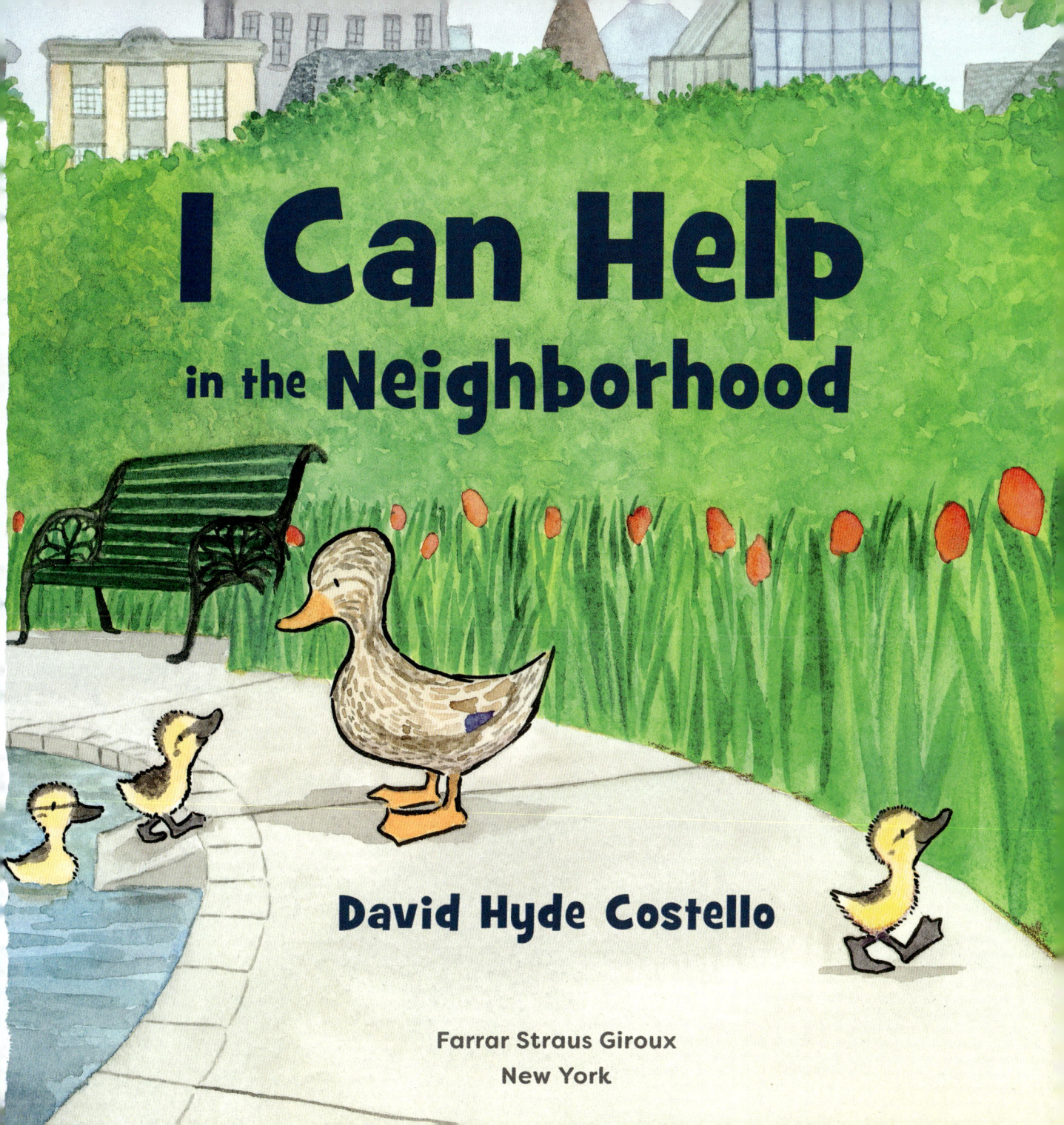
I Can Help
in the Neighborhood

David Hyde Costello

Farrar Straus Giroux
New York

For Eva

David Hyde Costello is the author and illustrator of *I Can Help* and *Here They Come!* He lives in Amherst, Massachusetts.

Farrar Straus Giroux Books for Young Readers
An imprint of Macmillan Publishing Group, LLC
120 Broadway, New York, NY 10271 • mackids.com

Copyright © 2024 by David Hyde Costello. All rights reserved.

Our books may be purchased in bulk for promotional, educational, or business use.
Please contact your local bookseller or the Macmillan Corporate and Premium Sales Department
at (800) 221-7945 ext. 5442 or by email at MacmillanSpecialMarkets@macmillan.com.

Library of Congress Control Number: 2023948312

First edition, 2024
Designed by Naomi Silverio
Color separations by Embassy Graphics
Printed in China by RR Donnelley Asia Printing Solutions Ltd.,
Dongguan City, Guangdong Province

ISBN 978-0-374-39133-1
1 3 5 7 9 10 8 6 4 2

Uh-oh. I'm lost.

I can help.

Thank you, rabbit!

Uh-oh. I'm tangled.

I can help.

Thank you, pigeon!

Uh-oh. I can't find cover.

I can help.

Uh-oh. I can't fit.

Thank you, rat!

Uh-oh. It's too heavy.

Uh-oh. Wet paint.

Thank you, duck!

Uh-oh. I'm lost again.